R. Johnson

GUESS WHO? MURDER IN A VILLAGE

AUSTIN MACAULEY PUBLISHERS®

LONDON • CAMBRIDGE • NEW YORK • SHARJAH

A CIP catalogue record for this title is available from the British Library.

ISBN 9781035876259 (Paperback)
ISBN 9781035876266 (Hardback)
ISBN 9781035876273 (ePub e-book)

www.austinmacauley.com

First Published 2024
Austin Macauley Publishers Ltd®
1 Canada Square
Canary Wharf
London
E14 5AA

Rebecca is an aspiring author who has been writing for many years. Due to her being dyslexic she has struggled with believing in herself and that her writing is good enough, but has continued to write anyway as Rebecca has found it therapeutic. Rebecca believes we all have a story in us but not all of them will get told.

Description

A murder takes place in a quiet village late at night. A newly appointed detective is sent to solve a case but quickly figures out there's a lot more going on in this village than meets the eye.

The detective with the help of their appointed officer, known as Officer Smith, has their work cut out. With a dead body, five witnesses, a Murderer to catch and a whole lot of questions to ask, does anyone fancy a game of Guess Who?

Chapter 1
Scene of the Crime

Late one night in a small village in the heart of the British countryside a murder takes place. While the innocent victim is being brutally and violently killed in her own home by someone they may or may not know, most of the villagers are at their local pub enjoying the evening and even making fools of themselves by competing in the pub quiz and giving the karaoke machine ago. While they laugh and joke with each other, make fun of the old drunk who's just fallen flat on his face. There were some villagers that didn't attend the pub that night. One was the nosey old lady who lives in the house across the street from where the murder is taking place. The old lady doesn't miss a thing when it comes to what goes on in the village on a day-to-day basis, as she is known for gossiping and people-watching all day and night. It came as a bit of a surprise the old lady didn't go to the pub that night, considering there's no better place to get the juiciest gossip than sitting quietly in the corner amongst a loud load of drunks, gossiping amongst themselves. Another villager missing that night was the window cleaner. A young man, who has just taken over his father's business was not at the pub that night either which was unusual for him as he is a regular. He is known to be a bit of a flirt and lady's man but has isolated himself as of late. The final person who wasn't seen that night was the shopkeeper. A young woman, and just like the window cleaner she's a regular at the local pub, but hasn't been as of late.

As the police arrive at the house, they slowly enter to find the young woman from the shop standing in the hallway with blood on her hands clearly in shock and staring into the room opposite. The officers approach slowly and ask the young woman, "Are you alright?" "Are you hurt?" the young woman struggling to speak just shakes her head and points into the room in front of her. The officers look through the door to see another young woman dead on the floor in between the sofa and table while walking towards the victim's body the officer calls through on the radio, "This is Officer Smith, we need backup here now a young woman in her late twenties possibly early thirties has been murdered, looks like she's been stabbed multiple times", "copy that officer, backups on its way". Office Smith looks at the other officer and says, "Stay with her, while I'll check the rest of the house." the officer responds with concern in his voice, "Do think that's wise, what if the murderers still hear" Officer Smith looks over at the officer as the officer indicates his comments were aimed at the young women "I just mean there's only two of us shouldn't we wait for backup and were not supposed to touch anything it's a crime scene", "I'm not going to touch anything, keep your cool" says Officer Smith, Officer Smith approaches the staircase and is about to walk up them, when suddenly a noise comes from the kitchen, Officer Smith rushes in only find the back door open with a smudged hand print on it and the victim's cat eating out of its food bowl. Officer Smith sighed with relief as the officer who was standing at the doorway asked, "Found anything" to which office Smith replied, "Not really, just the victim cat and a smudged handprint on the back door", Officer Smith returned to the hallway where the officer and the young women from the shop are, Officer Smith notices the young women has a cut on her right arm, not deep but deep enough for it to bleed through the sleeve of the top she is wearing.

It's now 01:40 am forensics has arrived at the crime scene and other officers are there as well to search the perimeter for any evidence. The young woman now in the back of an ambulance is being checked over by paramedics. After speaking with the forensics team. Officer Smith goes to check on the young woman and informs her that they will need her clothes as she could have sufficient evidence on her. The young woman seemed a bit hesitant and on edge about handing over her clothes that only seemed to have her own blood on them, even though Officer Smith started to get a bit suspicious about the young woman nonetheless, she got changed into the clothes that Officer Smith had given her. The final thing Officer Smith says to the young woman is, "The detective in charge will interview you, I hear the detective is very thorough so you better be ready for some intense questioning." Officer Smith walks away leaving the young woman now standing on the road staring at the victim's house as everyone from the pub comes over to find out what's going on. The police try to keep everyone calm while moving them on and telling them to go home but questions are still being asked by different villagers. One woman asks, "Has someone been hurt?" Another, "These types of things don't happen here, what's going on?" As the villagers start to leave and go home, most of them to sleep off the alcohol in their system. The detective who's been standing a few houses down from the crime scene observes the village and the people living in it. The detective notices the old lady sitting looking through her window, the young woman with tears running down her face visibly upset, the pub owner just standing at the doorway not bothered by the commotion, the window cleaner looking shifty and suspicious and finally the detective notices the gardener sat on the bench, the detective decides to walk over to the gardener and sits next to him, the detective just asks a simple question, "did you know the victim?" to which the gardener replied "yes" then paused before saying, "she's my ex". The detective slowly turns and looks at the gardener, looking the gardener up and down, examining the gardener looking for something anything except for the fact the gardener was visibly shaken and upset by the loss of his ex-partner the detective knew the first person you look at when a murder is committed especially the murder of a woman is the partner. The detective stood up turned to face the gardener and said, "I'm sorry for your loss, but I will need you to come to the station and give an interview." The detective paused for a moment and then said, "When you're ready". The detective turned and started walking back towards the house when the gardener shouted, "Why do I need to give an interview?" The detective stopped a smirk appeared on their face for a brief moment before the detective turned and said, "It's just routine, nothing to worry about," and carries on walking back to the house.

As the detective reaches the drive the young woman is still standing staring at the house, the detective stands next to her and says, "You've had difficulty evening" to which the young woman replies, "That's one way of putting it" she then looks to her left and says "I'm guessing you're the detective" to which the detective replies "you would guess correctly miss, you should go home and get some rest," the young women reply's "I think I might do that," the detective then says, "you should, you're going to need all the rest you can get," the detective pauses for a second before saying, "because I'm going to be interviewing you first miss, so I hope you've got your story straight." The young women didn't reply she just looked at the detective with a frown on her face and then turned her back on the detective and walked away.

In the detective's mind, they already had two suspects and they hadn't even entered the house yet to view the crime scene but as the detective walked towards the front door they came face to face with the two officers who were first on the scene. The detective stopped to speak with the officers. "morning officers", the detective said.

"Morning detective." The officers replied.

"I was told that you too were the first on the scene," the detective said.

"Yes detective," both officers replied.

"Now I need you to tell me everything from start to finish, don't leave anything out" the detective says.

"Best if you tell it," the officer says looking at Officer Smith.

The detective just looks at a very overwhelmed police officer and says, "First murder." The officer just nods his head "I can tell," the detective looks back over at Officer Smith and says, "Carry on", to which Officer Smith gives the details, "We received a call about midnight ("Midnight" says the detective) it takes about fifteen minutes to get hear ("so you would have arrived about 12:15, 12:20 at the latest" says the detective) when we arrived there was nobody around, not outside in the street, nothing it was like a ghost town ("except for that old lady watching from across the street," the officer chirps in) but with it being a Friday night everybody goes to the local pub ("clearly not everybody," says the detective) Officer Smith continues, "as we approached the house the front door was open slightly, as we entered the young women was stood in the hallway."

The detective interrupts, "Officer this next part I need you to be absolute with all the details of what you and your colleague saw."

Officer Smith replies, "I understand" then continues "We slowly approached the young woman asking her if she was alright or was she hurt, she seemed visibly shaken and in shock, the young woman was covered in blood, she pointed into the living room and that's when we saw the victim's body, I radioed it through straight away, there was nothing else out of the ordinary, it just looks like a straight forward murder" the detective smirks before replying "nothing in the criminal world officer is ever straightforward and you must never ever assume that it is" the detective continues "Alright officers, I appreciate the information, if there's anything else" Officer Smith interrupts the detective "actually, there is one other thing you should know" the detective looks at the officer waiting for the information "um… The young woman has a fresh cut on her right arm, it was still bleeding while we were waiting for backup up", the detective takes note thanks the officers for the information and tells them to go home and get some rest as they have a long road ahead of them into figuring this case out. The officers agree and leave the crime scene.

The detective proceeds into the house to finally see the crime scene for themselves. As the detective enters and walks down the hallway they notice something straight away, with the entrance to the kitchen being connected to the hallway, if the murderer was someone the victim didn't know she would have made an escape going for the back door and yet there are no blood stains or blood splatters in the hallway and therefore the murderer had to be someone she knew someone she trusted. As the detective was figuring all this out they turned to their left to see the victim's body lying on the floor in the living room, the detective sighed and whispered to themselves, "Hear we go again," a member of the forensics team comes over to the detective.

"So what we got this time," the detective says.

"Bit of a strange one if you ask me," says forensics.

"What do you mean?" says the detective.

"She has been stabbed twice, both times in the abdomen area, time of death between eleven and midnight, age late twenties early thirties," says forensics as he pauses before saying, "but that's it, there no sign of a struggle, nothing out of place or broken, it's like the murderer just walked in stabbed her and then left". The detective sighs and observes that there are two cups on the table, then says, "Found anything that could point towards the murderer," says the detective, "Truthfully, no we haven't," the forensics looks at the detective "but we are taking everything back to the lab" the detective replied, "good, keep me updated". The detective continues their search of the house, they enter the kitchen next, not that there's anything to see except for the back door being open and the smudged handprint on it. Clearly an adult size, the detective moves on upstairs asking the officers as they go if they've found anything to which each one has nothing to report. The detective notices a room at the end of the corridor and asks the officer if anyone has checked it yet to which the officer replies, "No, no one has been in there yet". The detective decides to go check it himself, the detective opens the door and Is shocked by what they see and so is the officer with them. Despite nearly everything packed away in boxes.

"It's a child's bedroom." The officer said.

"Yes, it is." The detective replied.

As the detective takes a look around the child's bedroom the detective comes across a photo. The child is a little boy and next to him in the photo is his father, the gardener, along with the victim. The question now is where was the little boy? That's something the detective would have to figure out and why did the house have such little furniture in it?

Chapter 2
The Shopkeeper

"Good morning," Officer Smith says with determination in her voice. "Morning all," the detective says as he walks into the office after a long night at the crime scene. "Have the forensics report been sent up yet?" the detective asks to which Officer Smith replies "No, not yet ". The detective decides to address the room.

"Listen up everyone, as you all know a young woman was murdered last night, In her own home," the detective continues, "Now while I'm waiting for the forensics report, we will start by elimination." The detective looks out at the room, "Officer Smith," the detective shouts.

"Yes, detective." Officer Smith replied.

"I want you to find out who wasn't at the pub last night, because whoever wasn't at the pub most likely won't have an alibi," the detective says with some determination.

"I'll get right on it," replies Officer Smith.

"As for the rest of you I won't all the information we can find on our victim and for now our number one suspect is currently the shopkeeper," the detective says.

Officers start gathering information on the victim first. A few hours later the detective comes out of his office and says,

"Right what information have you got for me". One by one the officers start to give what information they have on both the victim and the shopkeeper. The victim grew up in the village has lived there all her life, and went to school there. She and the gardener were high school sweethearts, they have a son together but she ended things with him after finding out he'd been having an affair with the pub owner. There were rumours that she'd started seeing somebody else and that her ex had become jealous and obsessed with finding out who it was. Another officer gives information on the shopkeeper, she also grew up here, went to the local school and was known to be close with the victim. Her brother is the window cleaner, one officer chirps up, "Small world", was a regular at the pub until recently. "interesting" the detective comments. Officer Smith returns from her investigation,

"I have news" Officer Smith says as she walks towards the board with all the current information the police have on it and pins up pictures of the villagers who don't have alibis.

"The people who were not at the pub last night are."

"The shopkeeper, which we already know."

"The old lady, who lives across from where the murder happened" and "the window cleaner".

"The gardener was seen at the pub last night but wasn't seen after ten-thirty".

The detective congratulates the officers for their hard work and asks the rest of the officers to start investing into each of them and look for any connections they may have to the victim. The detective turns to Officer Smith and asks her to go and collect the shopkeeper as it's time for her to be interviewed, the officer complies, "Right away detective".

Once Officer Smith returns and informs the detective the shopkeeper is in the interviewing room waiting, the detective invites Officer Smith with him to interview the shopkeeper. On their way down a member of the forensics team stops the detective to give him the report. The detective looks at the report and sees that there's nothing new in it but spots that the knife has not been found and none of the knives in the house are missing also more than one person entered the house that night. The detective also sees some relevant information which they decide to keep to themselves. The detective passes this information on to Officer Smith, as they continue to make their way to interview the shopkeeper the officer looks deep in thought before saying "More than one person entered the house, well we know one was the shopkeeper, the other must've been the murderer but more than one that could mean as many as four or more people went to that house last night".

As they reach the interviewing room, just before entering the detective turns to Officer Smith and says, "At the moment this case is completely wide open anyone could be the murderer, remember officer everyone is a suspect".

Both the detective and Officer Smith enter the room to start conducting the interview. As they entered, sat at the table with her lawyer the shopkeeper still looking visibly upset. Officer Smith and the detective both sit down at the table. The officer starts the interview, "interview begins at 02:15 pm".

The detective starts the interview with the first question "Miss, can you tell us what happened last night". The shopkeeper looked at the detective with the same frown on her face as she had last night when they first met as if she didn't trust the detective because the detective had already

made there mind up about her but replied softly with "alright"
The shopkeeper gives her version of events.

The shop closes at six, and by the time I've cashed up and tidied the shop I was probably finished about six thirty. I went straight home after that, I live a ten-minute walk away, so I got home for about quarter to seven, but by the time I'd had my tea and a shower it was pushing nine.

The detective jumps in, "As much as it's interesting to know your routine, what we need to know is what were you doing in the victim's house and how you got there".

The shopkeeper starting to look a bit on edge responds with "I don't know, I can't remember" ("That's not good enough" responds the detective) Officer Smith jumps in and asks "What's your relationship with the victim?" the shopkeeper looks at her lawyer and back at the detective and Officer Smith before answering very nervously "she was my partner" both the detective and Officer Smith look at each other in shock and disbelief before the detective says, "so you're the victim's secret partner." The shopkeeper responds "Yes, the only people who knew are my brother and that noise old lady, the gardener found out a few weeks ago." The detective responds with "ok, I need you to tell me what happened last night, the truth".

The shopkeeper starts again with her story. I always go around for about ten thirty, and the gardener picks his son up for the weekend at about eight. ("So the son is with his dad then" asks the detective) Yes, but only at the local pub, that's where the gardener lives, with the pub owner, she doesn't trust the gardener, thank god she never knew about the victim and I and he could never let go of the victim. That's why we were leaving the village, moving away and starting over. Get away from all the drama. "That explains the lack of furniture in the house." Officer Smith says, "Yes, we've slowly been packing and moving our stuff" replies the shopkeeper.

As Officer Smith was taking notes the detective asked another question on top of another question, "How did you cut your arm and where was your brother last night?"

The shopkeeper replies I don't know where my brother was last night, he was supposed to be at the pub keeping an eye on the gardener ("What do mean by that?" Officer Smith asks) that's how we were able to see each other without him causing any trouble, sometimes the gardener would take it upon himself to just show up at the house and they'd always end up arguing. The shopkeeper continues to talk but is getting more and more upset as she starts to talk about what happened just before the murder. "I thought it was him that showed up last night", the detective leans in and asks the shopkeeper to carry on.

"I went out through the back door and down to the shed that's next to the house, that's how I cut my arm, I caught it on a thorn bush there." The detective starts throwing questions at the shopkeeper, one after another.

"Did you see who it was?", "What time was it when they arrived at the house?", Officer Smith jumps in and says "Detective, I think you should let her speak" to which the detective replies, "Yes, of course, continue".

The shopkeeper clearly distressed continued, I didn't see who it was but they arrived just after half eleven, I didn't hear anything, I decided to start packing the shed up while I was in there, ("What were you doing in the shed" asks the detective) when the gardener comes round it's better if I'm out of the way, he doesn't kick off then, I waited for a bit then decided to look at my phone it said the time was five to twelve, I'd been outside for about twenty minutes at that point so I decided to go back in the house, I didn't realise at the time that I had cut my arm so the smudged hand print on the back door is mine, I quietly opened the door in case he was still there and as I walked through the kitchen into the hallway, I saw that the front door was open.

The shopkeeper barely held it together to describe the final part. I walked down the hallway turned into the living room and saw her lying there, I went over to her, and that's how I got her blood on me, then, I phoned for help.

Officer Smith while trying to take everything in just says "ok, miss thank you." The detective looking at the shopkeeper with a touch of sympathy in their eyes says, "Thank you for your cooperation you're free to go, for now", Officer Smith "The interview ended at 4:05 pm". The detective and Officer Smith leave the room and head back upstairs. On their way back, Officer Smith asks the detective his thoughts on what the shopkeeper had to say and whether or not he believes her.

"Do I believe she's innocent, no, do I believe her story, no?" says the detective. "why?" asks Officer Smith, "Why smith, yes the smudged hand print is hers forensics has confirmed that but her saying she did it coming back into the house doesn't go with the report."

"What does the report say?" asks Officer Smith, "it says a thorn was found in the right sleeve of her top, which would go with her story of how she says got the cut on her arm but the hand print on the back door was done by her left hand not her right."

They return to the office to find everyone busy at work. The detective enters their office followed by Officer Smith and with concern Officer Smith asks, "What do you think the chances are that we catch this murder." The detective after a long day sighs, looks at Officer Smith and replies, "Truthfully, at this very moment in time we have nothing, no murder weapon, no witnesses, not even a scrap of hair to go by officer, all we have are four people who don't have alibi's and we have to ask questions and figure out who did it" the detective walks over to the office window looking out at the evidence board covered with suspects faces, then turns and looks back at Officer Smith and says "so officer, fancy a game of Guess Who?".

Chapter 3
The Window Cleaner

The next day Officer Smith arrives at the station early, only to find that the detective is already in the office standing staring at the evidence board but most noticeable at the victim's picture.

"You're here early," says Officer Smith, taken by surprise the detective responds with just, "So are you". As Officer Smith proceeds to her desk she notices the detective in a different mood today, than he was in yesterday. Officer Smith decides to walk over to the detective and view the evidence board. After taking their time viewing all the evidence gathered (which isn't much apart from photos of suspected suspects) Officer Smith asks the detective what's bothering him, indicating that they seem to be in a bad mood.

"What do you expect," the detective snaps back at the officer "A woman's been murdered and we have nothing but the dead body, we've already interviewed our main suspect and walked away with pretty much nothing except for the fact that she was in a relationship with the victim" the officer stood leaning against one of the desks, watching on as the detective continues to let out their frustrations over the difficulties of this case so far.

Once finished the officer just looks at the detective and says "better" to which the detective just smiles and says "yes, much better". The detective now feeling more motivated than ever pin points what they believe to be important information from the interview with the shopkeeper.

- The shopkeeper was in a relationship with the victim
- Claims someone came to the house between eleven thirty and midnight while she was in the garden shed, where she claims to have cut her arm on a thorn bush
- Admits the smudged handprint on the back door is hers
- Also claims to be the one who called the police

The detective indicates that this is all the relevant information from the interview with the shopkeeper. As the detective and Officer Smith are finishing up with their notes, all the other officers start to arrive. "good morning everyone" the detective says just before he addresses the room. As the detective is about to address the officers working on the case and update them on any new information, the detective gets called over by one of the officers from reception, the detective leaves Officer Smith in charge of the meeting. The detective walks over and asks the officer what the urgency is to which the officer responds by telling the detective that the window cleaner is downstairs requesting to speak with him, the detective surprised by this development tells the officer, "Put him in one of the interviewing rooms and I'll be down now," to which the officer just nods there head in acknowledgement and leaves. The detective returns to the meeting as it is finishing and informs Officer Smith of the developments to

Officer Smith's surprise. She questions why the window cleaner has come to the station and requests to speak with the detective. Before the detective leaves to interview the window cleaner he says to Officer Smith, "It will be interesting to see what the brother has to say, another one without an alibi".

The detective leaves to go and interview the window cleaner. Just before the detective enters the interviewing room, Officer Smith catches up and says, "Not without me" before opening the door to see a young man sitting behind the table.

The interview starts with the detective asking the window cleaner why he's taken it upon himself to go to see them, to which the window cleaner responds by saying, "I wanted to get my side of the story told first before that waste of space tries to blame everything on me" to which both the detective and Officer Smith look at the window cleaner with confusion as he continues "that gardener thinks I'm the one who killed her, me" The detective determined to make sure they ask all the relevant questions this time, interrupts and starts with the first question "what was your relationship with the victim?" to which the window cleaner replies, "she was my sister's partner".

"where were you the night of the murder?", the window cleaner hesitates "I was out of town". Officer Smith jumps in "Where out of town and who with?", the window cleaner sat with his arms crossed and legs shaking, "I was on my way back from a friend's and decided to drive around for a bit" The detective looking at the window cleaner who's sat right across from them "what time did you leave you friends and what time did you get back". The window cleaner desperately tries to come up with an alibi but the detective can see straight through him "Enough, you don't have an alibi" the window cleaner tries arguing back but the detectives not having any of it "No you don't, everything you're telling us, your making up as you go along, I am many things but an idiot isn't one of them". The detective takes a breath and sits back in the chair before saying "You're going to tell me where you were and what happened the night of the murder or I will arrest you for wasting police time". The window cleaner just nods his head and complies before saying "ok" giving his version of events.

The window cleaner starts but gets to the point quickly. "I finished work at four, went straight home to have something to eat and to get changed before making, the two-hour drive to go and visit my father who's currently serving a five-year sentence in prison" as the detective goes to ask a question the Window Cleaner jumps over them, "I got there for about six thirty was with my father for an hour then drove back, stopped at a local service station on the way so I probably got back about ten and went straight to bed".

"What's your father in prison for" Officer Smith asks. The window cleaner looks up at the officer, leans on the table and says, "A few weeks ago after the gardener found out about my sister and the victim, he went to the local shop and started threatening my sister, he even grabbed her by the arm and told her to stay away from the victim, my father went mad and beat the crap out of the gardener but he did it in the wrong place" ("what you mean" asks the detective) "he did it outside the local pub, the pub owner called the police and my father got charged with assault" ("what were you expecting, that your father would get away it" says the detective). The window cleaner responds with intent "the pub owner only did it to please the gardener and once I've finished telling you their history you'll understand why we hate each other". The interview goes on for another hour, the window cleaner explaining how the gardener's affair with the pub owner was over months ago and how he'd been trying to win the victim back ever since, leaving the pub owner looking embarrassed and like a fool after she went round the village flaunting their affair and rubbing it in the victim's face, only for the gardener to suddenly drop her and tell her he'd made a massive mistake and after the gardener found out about his sister and the victim and there plans to move away, he got back with the pub owner "I wouldn't be surprised if he didn't do it, kill her, if he hadn't had that affair his jealousy would've ended their relationship", "I am surprised she had him back, she's not the type of person you want to cross". Once the interview is over the window cleaner is free to go.

After returning to the office, Officer Smith starts putting together relevant information and evidence from their interview with the Window cleaner and asks one of the officers to check his alibi about visiting his father in prison the night of the murder. The detective, who has been holding something back from everyone, decides to go back through the forensics report and as the detective is reading they once again whisper to themselves, "This isn't looking good for you gardener". The detective writes down relevant information about the window cleaner.

- Possible alibi before the murder
- No alibi for the time of the murder
- Doesn't get on with the gardener

There's a knock on the door and an officer enters the detective's office to inform them that the window cleaner was indeed visiting his father the night of the murder. The detective gets up from their chair and walks out of their office to address the room.

"listen up everyone" the detective shouts. As the detective informs every one of the latest developments there are discussions in the room about what information they have so far who could possibly be the murderer. One officer suggests that it could be both the brother and sister who are the murderers as the window cleaner doesn't have an alibi for the time of the murderer and the sister was found with the victim's blood on her. Another suggestion is it looks more like the gardener, with his desperate attempts to win back the victim and his jealous behaviour could very well be a motive.

The detective reminds everyone that while their enthusiasm is welcomed they still haven't interviewed the gardener yet or the old lady and as the meeting comes to an end, Officer Smith returns and informs the detective that they got word the son was staying at the pub the night of the murder. "At least we now know where he was that night," the detective replies walking back to his office, followed by Officer Smith, "What now?" asks Officer Smith. The detective sits in his chair leaning back in it, looking at the paperwork on their desk, all of it to do with the case. "We still have two people to interview who don't have alibis", the detective picks up a folder that's lying on their desk, "But I have to admit it's looking more and more like the gardener is guilty", "and if he isn't" Officer Smith replies. As the detective puts the file back down on their desk, he looks at

Officer Smith and says with some concern, "Then someone's going to a lot of trouble to make him look guilty."

As Officer Smith goes to leave the detective's office she makes a suggestion about looking into the pub owner, even though she claims to have an alibi, it wouldn't hurt to check her out. The detective pauses for a moment before agreeing with Officer Smith saying it might even be worth interviewing her at some point. what was it the window cleaner said, "She's not the type of person you want to cross" As Officer Smith left she turned and said, "I'll get onto it first thing tomorrow," and shut the office door behind them, leaving the detective in deep thought.

Chapter 4
A Second Victim

It's the following day the detective who's spent all night at the station receives news that there's been another murder in the village. When the detective asks who the victim is the officer tells him that it's the old lady. As the detective starts walking out to head to the crime scene the same officer shouts "Officer Smith is already there" but the detective just carries on walking.

Once back in the village and at the old lady's house which has now become the new crime scene, the detective once again stands and looks around, this time it's in daylight instead of the middle of the night. The detective can't help but look at the first victim's house which is right opposite. Looking back towards the old lady's house the detective notices the window cleaner and the shopkeeper standing in their garden, a few doors down, the shopkeeper looking a shell of herself and the window cleaner looking heartless as well as the pub owner once again not bothered by the events.

A lot of the villagers (this time sober) are once again asking questions but are more aggressive and impatient to the point that the detective has to intervene this time and say something. The detective addresses everyone's concerns and assures them that there doing everything they can. One villager shouts, "No you're not," another "Are we even safe?" With more and more questions being shouted, the detective's impatience kicks in and says to the officer next to them, "I don't have time for this, deal with it please" the officer nods and proceeds to interact with villagers, which gives the detective the opportunity to leave and carry on into the old lady's house.

Once inside the detective meets Officer Smith and a member of the forensics team at the bottom of the stairs. Officer Smith informs the detective that just like the first victim, the murderer had to be someone the old lady knew, as the front door was unlocked and once again left open. The detective asks where the murder took place and Officer Smith states it took place in the old lady's bedroom, the detective asks to be shown to the crime scene to which Officer Smith shows the detective the way.

As they head up the stairs the forensics team member informs the detective that the old lady was killed by being stabbed once in the chest from behind and that this time they have a knife. Once in the old lady's bedroom, the detective notices that she was sitting in her chair in front of the window with the perfect view of the village and the first victim's house and could see who would've been coming and going from that house on an everyday basis especially the night of the murder.

The detective walks over to where the old lady is, standing In front of her the detective crouches down. The forensics team member asks the detective what he is doing as everything has already been checked over for evidence, the detective wearing gloves spots something and carefully picks up what looks like the corner of an envelope and gently pulls it from underneath the old lady's chair and says to the forensics team member clearly not. The detective stands back up looks at the envelope and sees that it has, "To The Detective" written on the front. Officer Smith says, "Do you think she saw who it was and she wrote it all down".

"I think we shouldn't jump to conclusions officer, this letter may contain the answer but it may also be a confession" says the detective.

"A confession, the woman's been killed and your theory is she wrote a confession and then stabbed herself" Officer Smith replies with a sarcastic tone in her voice, the detective looks at Officer Smith with amusement and as the detective starts to walk away, handing the envelope found to the forensics team member to be examined and making clear once all the tests have been done it's to be returned to the detective immediately to which the forensics team member complies.

The detective tells Officer Smith their theory, "My theory, officer, is the old lady knew that the murderer was coming for her, that's why she possibly left the front door unlocked, to allow the murderer to let themselves in, walk up the stairs and kill her" Officer Smith asks "why would the old lady do that" to which the detective answers "My guess is, the old lady staying sat in her chair, she could see the murderer coming and that possibly gave her time to not only write that letter but to hide it". After exiting the old lady's house the detective decides before returning to the station to visit the local pub. Since it's just up the road the detective decides to walk there and time themselves doing it. Once at the pub, the detective checked his watch and saw that it took him less than ten minutes to get there, which means if it was the gardener or anyone else from the pub that night they would had to of left before half eleven to walk to the victim's house to commit the murder and get back before the police arrived. The detective realises if it was someone from the pub that night they only would've had a fifteen-minute window to commit the murder and leave before the shopkeeper entered the house. As the detective enters the pub the gardener is sitting at the bar, next to him is his son who is busy colouring and standing behind the bar is the pub owner, who has a similar look to the shopkeeper but is clearly older.

The pub owner immediately acting defensively asks what the detective wants, to which the detective makes clear that he's only there to remind the gardener that he still has to go to the station to give an interview. The gardener makes it clear that he hasn't forgotten but can't while he has no one to watch his son. To which the detective asks why the pub owner can't keep an eye on the boy considering the two of them are in a relationship, to which the gardener snaps back at the detective and says he'll come and give the interview when he can and that he's got nothing to hide. It's at this point the gardener's son turns and looks at the detective and then at both the pub owner and the gardener who at this point had walked around the bar and was stood next to the pub owner and then the boy carries on colouring. As the detective goes to leave they tell the gardener he has until the end of the week to come to the station and give an interview otherwise there will be a warrant out for his arrest, to which the gardener just tells the detective to do what he wants. Outside the pub, the detective tries to understand what he has just witnessed thinking to themselves that wasn't a happy situation let alone a relationship.

While the detective is deep in thought Officer Smith with one of the girls from the village comes over, Officer Smith tells the young girl that this is the detective she wanted to speak to and the young girl tells the detective that she works in the pub, behind the bar and informs the detective that the only time the gardener left the bar was to go and check on his son about ten thirty but never came back and that she didn't see him again until they were all outside the victim's house, the detective asks about the pub owner and if she ever left during the evening to which the young girl replies by telling the detective that she did to go and change some of the barrels the detective asks what time, the young girl implies that it was between eleven and eleven-thirty but didn't notice how long she was gone or what time she returned, only that it was just before everyone in the pub left to go and see what was going on outside.

The young girl leaves and as the detective and Officer Smith go to get in the car they notice the pub owner standing on the steps outside the pub, she asks the detective how she knows he thinks it is the gardener and they'd be right to think that, the detective walks back over to the pub owner followed by Officer Smith and asks her why, to which she replies "well, with the victim being pregnant he was never going to let her leave, let alone allow someone else to bring that child up", the detective just thanks the pub owner for the information and gets in the car and drives away.

Back at the station Officer Smith asks the detective if they're going to discuss what the pub owner revealed about the victim. The detective inside his office with Officer Smith decides to close the door and tell Officer Smith that he knew about the victim being pregnant all this time because it was in the report but kept the information to themselves especially from any of the suspects because the detective wanted to see who new and which one of them would slip up first. Officer Smith clearly upset with the detective for holding back information just looks at the detective and asks what's next. The detective continues by laying it all out there saying how from the start they believed it was the gardener but so far there's nothing to prove that it was and also points out that it wasn't the gardener who slipped up with the victim being pregnant it was the pub owner as well as the fact there's new evidence that proves the pub owner doesn't have an alibi for the time of the first murder, so they now have a new suspect.

The detective sat in his chair tells Officer Smith, I think we can narrow down who are murderer is to just two people either the gardener who everyone describes as jealous and obsessed with the first victim or the pub owner someone who was humiliated and embarrassed by the gardener so decided to get revenge.

Officer Smith looking at the Detective agrees but insinuates there's nothing they can do until they get the report back about the old lady's murderer not that there's going to be anything new in it but most importantly the letter, so they can find out what the old lady wrote to the detective and what she saw that night, if she saw anything at all.

The detective stands up from his desk and insists there is one thing for them to do while they wait for the report and the old lady's letter to be returned and that is to interview the gardener about the night of the first murderer, as the detective opens there office door to go and start the meeting with the other officers, Officer Smith asks if the detective thinks the gardener will come of his own accord as the detective starts to walk out of there office they look back at office one and replies "I've got a feeling he will, now we have a meeting to do come on".

After the meeting is over and for the time everyone's attention is now on the gardener and the pub owner as they have become the main suspects, the detective discusses the gardener's son with Officer Smith and how he looked scared when looking at his father and the pub owner earlier in the day. Officer Smith tells the detective to expect the boy to be quiet and fearful after all his mothers been murdered and his father is a suspect, the poor boy is not going to want to talk to anyone Officer Smith says. The detective thinking about the case replies, "Maybe he knows something and that's why" Officer Smith while walking back to their desk sighs and answers, "Maybe, maybe not, you seriously be thinking of interviewing a child." The detective replies, "If I have to, I will," and walks back to their office closing the door behind them.

Chapter 5
The Gardener

The next day at the station the detective arrives to find Officer Smith going back through all the evidence, curious the detective walks over to Officer Smith and asks if they've found anything new. To which the officer, taken by surprise just shakes her head, the detective responds with a simple and sharp response, "Thought not." The detective then persists to his office as Officer Smith continues with their reading.

Later in the morning Officer Smith carrying on with her research decides to look into the pub owner, with the detective busy in his office and obviously not in a very good mood as the gardener still hasn't shown up to be interviewed yet, decides not to bother the detective until she has something concrete and worth interrupting the detective.

A few hours into their research, Officer Smith has so far come across nothing worthwhile about the pub owner, all the information the officer could find out about her is that she bought the pub a few years ago, is still married and has two children. Officer Smith decides to dig a bit deeper into the pub owner and finds out that her ex-husband has filed for divorce because of her affair with another man, a younger man. As the officer continues to dig deeper into the pub owner's past they find out that there's more going on here than meets the eye.

With the new information Officer Smith has just discovered and the importance of it she decides the detective needs to know and the sooner the better. Officer Smith gets up from her desk and starts walking towards the detective's office with determination, determination to inform the detective of what she has just discovered but as Officer Smith arrives at the detective's office, the detective isn't in there and Officer Smith turns and looks around the room to see if the detective is somewhere only to stop an officer walking past and ask them where the detective is as they have some really important information to tell the detective, the officer informs Officer Smith the detective has gone downstairs to interview the gardener, Officer Smith surprised that the detective didn't ask her to join him to interview the gardener, decides to wait till the detective gets back to inform him of the information they have found. Downstairs the detective has arrived to interview the gardener. As the detective is about to walk in the room they notice the gardener's son sitting in the waiting area, the detective tells the officer behind the desk to make sure the boy is alright and that if he wants anything he has it, to which the officer complies.

The detective enters the room to find the gardener impatiently sitting waiting to be interviewed, as the detective takes a seat the gardener starts by saying that he hasn't got all day, to which the detective very quickly responds by saying "I'll take as long as I need to, since you've kept us waiting", The gardener just looks at the detective and smirks before saying "point taken" leaning back in the chair.

The detective looks at the gardener and says, "Now, let's get started". The detective begins by asking the gardener about his relationship with the victim to which the gardener explains that there was nothing wrong with their relationship and how it was perfect, how they were happy and comfortable with their life. The detective then asks if his life was so good why did he have an affair with the pub owner, to which the gardener explains to the detective it was never anything serious it was always just a bit of fun and despite how perfect his life at the time was with the victim as well as how much he loved her, he missed going out and having fun.

The detective moves on to the victim's relationship with the shopkeeper. The detective asks why the gardener threatened the shopkeeper after finding out about her relationship with the victim. The gardener laughs before saying, "Threatened, is that what they told you", the gardener continues to explain how he went to see the shopkeeper after finding out about their relationship to make sure the shopkeeper wasn't doing it out of revenge but that nosey old lady was in the shop at the time and went straight back and told the shopkeepers brother everything. The detective asks the gardener what he means by that, it's then the gardener reveals to the detective that the shopkeeper and the window cleaner are the pub owner's children and after he made it perfectly clear their affair was nothing but a bit of fun, the window cleaner has had it in for him ever since and that he blames him for his father being in prison, the gardener explains.

The detective surprised by this news asks the gardener if he knew the victim was pregnant, to which the gardener reveals that he did and despite all the rumours of him being jealous and controlling, the gardener wanted nothing more than the victim and his son away from the village, as he feared either the window cleaner or at worst the pub owner would do something if they stayed. "After the window cleaner, beat me up and allowed his father to take the blame I wouldn't put anything past him," The detective asks the gardener where he was at the time of the murder, and the gardener responds by saying he doesn't have an alibi, I was downstairs in the pub until ten thirty and then I went to check on my son and I decided to stay upstairs and watch TV until everything kicked off.

The detective with one final question asks if the gardener thought the shopkeeper's relationship with the victim was genuine or just an act of revenge on her mother's behalf to which the gardener insinuates that he believes their relationship was genuine and she wanted out from under her mother but as for the window cleaner, he's close with his mother and tells her everything, she probably already knew about their relationship and about the victim being pregnant before me, says the gardener.

The gardener also informs the detective he was with his son the night of the old lady's murder, they were watching a film and that the shopkeeper was there as well, she's been spending a lot of time at the pub again. The detective ends the interview and tells the gardener that's all for now and that he may want to speak to him again, to which the gardener just nods in acceptance and asks to be taken to his son to which the detective complies and tells the officer to release the gardener.

Once the gardener has left the detective stops the recording and is left alone in the interviewing room with their head in their hands, trying to understand and make sense of all this mess and family drama, a family drama which has been the cause of two murders and what for, the detective asking themselves is this really a case where someone has committed a murder out of revenge or embarrassment and then committed a second to try and cover up the first. The detective looking at the file in front of him with all the evidence collected so far,

- The shopkeeper at the scene of the first murder, covered in the victim's blood and the one who called the police and has an alibi for the old lady's murder
- The window cleaner with no alibi at the time of the first murder
- The gardener with no alibi for the time of the first murder and claims he was with his son at the time of the old lady's murder

The detective leaves the interview room and heads back upstairs to find Officer Smith waiting for him in their office looking impatient, as the detective enters his office, Officer Smith immediately starts to inform the detective of the information she has discovered and the detective stops the officer and tells her that he already knows about how the window cleaner and the shopkeeper are the pub owners children to which Officer Smith asks how the detective found out and the detective replies by telling the officer that the gardener told him everything in the interview, well the detective thinks he told him everything anyway.

Officer Smith asks the detective what the next move is to which the detective replies by asking if the forensics report has been brought up along with the letter they found, to which the officer says, "Nothing's been brought in while I've been sat here waiting for you. The detective frustrated tells Officer Smith that there are no close to finding the murderer and that they definitely have two possible suspects.

- The window cleaner
- The gardener

Officer Smith also indicates that there very well might be a chance that the pub owner is a suspect too and should be interviewed, to which the detective with all the information they have agrees, thinking she could very well have a motive for murder, especially if it's a murder out of revenge.

As the detective is planning their next move with Officer Smith, there's a knock on the door and into the office comes the detective's superior, "Detective, I wonder If I might have a word" to which the detective complies and Officer Smith mutters "I'll just… go… and look into something," as they leave the detectives office, closing the door behind them.

Inside the detective's office, the detective is arguing with his superior over the lack of action being taken as well as progress in these two murder cases. The superior informs the detective that the pressure is pilling on to find who is responsible, not just from the villagers who want answers but from the media as well, "I know you're doing your best with what you have but time is running out detective, solve this case and fast." The superior officer leaves the detectives office and walks out with the whole room in silence looking at each other and then at the detective's office.

A few moments later the detective appears and holds a meeting with everyone to inform them of what the superior officer had to say and some of the officers are not happy about it, leading to some sarcastic comments, "What they expect to happen, the murderer to hand themselves in" and another "or to give us a helping hand by leaving actual evidence so we can find them" and one final comment came from Officer Smith "the villagers have a cheek anyway, so far none of them have been honest with us so why should we keep them updated". The detective takes in all of the comments made and makes one final announcement before sending everyone home, "I'm glad you are all as angry and frustrated as I am because tomorrow we're going to take every scrap of evidence we have and go back to the beginning, we are going to paint a picture of what we think possible happened that night which I believe will help point us in the right direction, now go home and get some rest, got a busy day tomorrow".

All the officers agree with the detective and leave the office understanding that tomorrow they will have a better picture of what happened and who they are looking for. Will returning to the beginning help the detective solve this case? Or is the detective just going around in circles?

Chapter 6
Back to The Start

It's the following day and everyone is at the office early keen on getting started. The detective who still doesn't understand what taking the forensics team so long with the report decides to send someone down to find out, in the meantime the detective addresses the room and asks if everyone is ready to piece together what they have so far to give them a better picture of the events that took place that night. All of the officers gather around, They start with the shopkeeper's record of events, The detective puts together what they have "So, the shopkeeper claims she arrived at the victim's house at about ten thirty, they were together for about an hour before someone arrived at the house", the detective continues "the shopkeeper said in her interview that they thought it might have been the gardener, so to prevent any arguments she decided to go and hid in the shed, where she cut her arm and waited twenty minutes before returning to the house to find the victim". One of the officers interrupts "that's a good alibi even plausible, you could say" the officer a bit hesitant it what there about say but the detective encourages them to speak "It's just, the shopkeepers story about going and hiding in the shed, doesn't make sense, why not just hid upstairs?", the detective says to the officer "good point and good question, officer" the detective replies. They accept the shopkeeper does have an alibi for the time of the old lady's murder as long as what the gardener has said is true. Another officer indicates that the shopkeeper is unlikely to be the murderer to which the detective replies, "How's that officer." The officer gives their theory of why would the shopkeeper murder her own partner when she was about to start a new life with her "True, but that doesn't mean she isn't hiding something, she may still know more about that night than what she's told us, we may need to speak to her again" the detective tells the officer. The detective decides to move on to the window cleaner, which is a short story. "Got back from visiting his father about ten and that's it, has no alibi for the time of both murders", to which one of the officers replies, "I think we have our murderer", the detective looks back at the room "I would like to think so officer but unfortunately even though he doesn't have an alibi, without evidence to back it up, it's just a theory, moving on". They continue with the gardener next and again he hasn't got an alibi for the time of the murder but does have one for the old lady's murder but will need the shopkeeper or at most his son to back him up on it and finally the pub owner who has yet to be interviewed has already had evidence given against her by one of her own employees, telling the detective that she left the bar between eleven and half eleven and didn't notice when she returned. The detective pleased with everyone's hard work and input, realises their number one suspect is the Window Cleaner, who clearly has no alibi for either murder and that they need to interview the pub owner and find out where she was during the time of the murder and re-interview the shopkeeper as her story doesn't quite add up. The detective also realises they may even need to speak to the gardener's son but wants to leave that as a last resort. Once the meeting is over the detective goes to find out if the officer he sent down to the forensics department had any luck in finding out what's going on with the report and the letter they found at the old lady's house. The officer informs the detective that the report is on his desk along with the old lady's letter, ready for him to view, the detective asks the officer if they found out what took so long with the report and the officer just shrugs his shoulders and says "I asked but they never gave me a reason", the detective then carries on to their office to look through the report.

The detective starts reading through the report not expecting there to be anything they don't already know to be there. As time goes by and the further the detective reads into the report it's just more of the same but the detective notices that the knife left at the crime scene and used to kill the old lady was a different one compared to the type of knife used on the victim and the detective wonders why?

Was it to make the detective think there are two murderers to catch, was it to try and trick the detective or was the murderer just simply playing games or has the murderer had enough and wanted to be caught? There were no fingerprints found on the knife which means the killer was wearing gloves, therefore the detective is left with more questions than answers once again and his frustrations start to grow, just as the detective thought he was getting somewhere, it feels like he is still standing still. The detective sees that the forensics team has left a note in the report for the detective informing him why the report took so long.

Detective,

Sorry, the report took so long but as you may know, we didn't just examine the letter that was found, we also had to check to make sure it was not a fake or a fraud, so whatever the old lady wrote you would be able to use as evidence.

We can confirm that this letter was indeed written by the old lady herself and therefore you can use it as evidence in your case.

Yours sincerely
The forensics team

Before the detective decides to read the old lady's letter she had left for him, the detective calls Officer Smith into his office. Officer Smith enters and takes a seat, asking the detective if everything is alright the detective informs the officer of the report and asks for her thoughts.

Officer Smith starts off by saying to the detective, "I can tell you what I think happened and who I think did it if you'll listen," to which the detective sits back in there chair looks at Officer Smith and says, "Go on then" and it's then Officer Smith gives their thoughts, "I believe what the shopkeeper has told us but I don't believe she went outside to hide, I believe she was running from the murder.

"The cut on her arm wasn't done by a thorn bush," the officer continues, "I think the shopkeeper was in the house at the time the murderer arrived, she might not have been in the same room when the murder was taking place but I believe she was there and walked in on the murder", the detective just looking at Officer Smith and nodding, Officer Smith out of frustration shouts at the detective that this has already been pointed out to them by other officers but hasn't taken it into consideration because they've been so fixated on the old lady's letter.

The detective decides to remind the officer of the difficulties and pressures that they are under in finding the person responsible and how if they don't, all the officers working on this case won't be the ones that reap the consequences and won't have to face there superior or the villagers and media and explain how they have allowed a murderer to get away with killing two people and how that responsibility falls on the detective. "So if it looks like I care more about a dame letter right now officer that is because it's the only piece of evidence we have right now, that just might identify our murderer," the detective sighs.

"But considering you seem so interested in the shopkeeper story, why don't you go and interview her," Officer Smith gets up from her chair, "Yes, detective," the officer replies and leaves the detective's office to go and re-interview the shopkeeper.

Officer Smith arrives back in the village and at the shopkeeper's house, as she goes to knock on the door Officer Smith can hear the shopkeeper arguing with someone, so she decides to try and listen in to see if she can hear what's being said, "As long as you stick to your story everything will be fine," as the voices are getting closer, Officer Smith hears the shopkeeper saying "everything will be fine, my life's been ruined", with the shopkeeper and her guest just the other side of the door Officer Smith doesn't want them to know she's been listening and knocks on the door in a panic.

The door opens and it's the pub owner on the other side surprised Officer Smith asks for the shopkeeper to which the shopkeeper invites the officer in and says that her mother was just going, the pub owner looks at her daughter and says, "Remember what I said," and then leaves.

Officer Smith enters the shopkeeper's house and tells her that the detective sent her to ask some questions, "more questions" the shopkeeper implies, "unfortunately, yes" the officer replies. As they sit in the living room Officer Smith tells the shopkeeper that they just need her to clarify she was with the gardener and his son watching a film the night the old lady got murdered "Yes, we're at the pub that night, we were watching a film the gardener invited me over he thought it would be good for me to spend some time with his son, neither of us left."

Officer Smith then asks the shopkeeper, "One final thing, out of curiosity, the night of the murder, why did you go outside to hide and not upstairs," The shopkeeper not knowing what to say, "It was a question which was raised", Officer Smith casually replies the shopkeeper struggling to get her words out replies "I was in the kitchen at the time, so I just went straight out the back door", not believing a word Officer Smith just nods and says "alright" and moves on.

After a while Officer Smith decides to leave and return to the station, Officer Smith reminds the shopkeeper that if she remembers anything else or changes her mind about anything she knows where they are, the shopkeeper acknowledges the officer as she leaves the house. Once outside the officer notices the village seems to be a bit quiet for the middle of the day, Officer Smith notices the window cleaner out the corner of her eye lurking down by the side of the pub, wondering has he been there watching the entire time, she's been with the shopkeeper. Officer Smith leaves and heads back to the station to report to the detective what she has found out and to see if the detective is in a better mood. On her way back to the station Officer Smith can't help but wonder what the shopkeeper is hiding. And what was the conversation with her mother about?

Chapter 7
The Old Lady's Letter

Back at the station the detective is about to read the letter left by the old lady but is unsure about what will be in it, will it be a confession or the evidence the detective desperately needs? The detective carefully takes the letter out of the evidence bag, holding it in his hands gently and delicately so as to not get anything on it that could affect it in any way, as the detective starts to read.

Dear Detective,

I know by the time you get this I will no longer be with you. As you have been told by now probably by many of the villagers, I am nothing but the nosey old lady who likes to gossip but the truth is detective when one is as old and alone as I am you seek interaction from others even if it's just a hello how are you? And yes, gossiping about others comes in handy. Anyway, I know what you're thinking reading this, you're hoping I can tell you who killed that poor woman and the truth is, I can't but I can help you narrow it down to just two people. I know a lot of people think it's the gardener but I promise you detective despite all the horrible things you've been told about him, It was not the gardener. The gardener picked his son up at the usual time and had a short chat with the victim probably about the baby and how she was feeling, like I said, despite the horrible rumours that the window cleaner had said, about how the gardener was jealous of the victim and the shopkeeper, it was quite the opposite. He had accepted his mistake and just wanted what was best for his family.

Can't say the same about the window cleaner mind you, if there's anyone who is jealous and controlling it's him, he's wanted revenge on the gardener ever since he dumped his mother and it got worse when he found out, not only that they got back together but that his sister was with the victim, the things he has done. Beating up the gardener and getting his own father to take the blame and then even threatening his own sister in the shop when his mother told him about her relationship with the victim and saying it was the gardener and I knew the only reason the shopkeeper went along with it, is because she's scared of her brother.

Anyway the night of the murder I decided to stay home, I hadn't been well recently and didn't fancy being around all those two-faced idiots. The gardener came at the normal time to pick up his son left and returned to the pub and then the window cleaner arrived back at ten, probably from visiting his father but he wasn't in a good mood, he went straight into the house, he and his sister live in. Half an hour later I saw the shopkeeper arriving at the victim's house, after that I must have dozed off because the next thing I knew it was 11:40 and the window cleaner was sitting on the doorstep of the victim's house and it looked like he was tying his shoe laces, before leaving, walking what looked like in the direction of the pub. it wasn't until the police arrived and I found out that poor girl had been murdered that I realised that the killer had to be either the window cleaner or the shopkeeper but to be perfectly honest with you detective I would bet my life that the window cleaner is responsible for that poor girl's death.

I'm sorry I can't be any more help to you detective, I just hope you find this letter in time.

After reading the old lady's words for themselves the detective realises that with this letter there is convincing evidence along with the fact the window cleaner doesn't have an alibi for the times of both murders, to say that they have found their murderer but the most difficult part now is proving it. The detective while waiting for Officer Smith to return decides to inform the rest of the officers working on the two cases and asks them to focus their attention on the window cleaner and the pub owner.

Once Officer Smith arrives back at the station and is informed that the detective wishes to see her, the officer then heads to the detective's office. After entering the office, Officer Smith informs the detective of what they heard when they arrived at the shopkeeper's house.

"detective, you'll never guess what I overheard when I arrived at the shopkeeper's house", the detective interested in what a very enthusiastic Officer Smith had to say and waits for the officer to continue, "As I was about knock on the door, I overheard someone say to the shopkeeper, as long as you stick to your story, everything will be fine", and Officer Smith explains how the shopkeeper sounded like she was being forced if not pressured into lying about the night of murder in order to protect someone.

Officer Smith continued telling the detective that the person who had been having this conversation with the shopkeeper was the pub owner, explaining she was the one to open the front door to Officer Smith and leave but before she did Officer Smith told the detective, "the last thing she said to her daughter was, remember what I said, and left".

The detective intrigued by this asks Officer Smith if there was anything else they found out before informing the officer what was in the old lady's letter and how not only do they now know who the killer most likely is but that they have the most difficult part of proving it.

"That's interesting information officer, did you find anything else out while you were in the village", the detective asks and Officer Smith surprised by the detective's interest pauses for a moment before answering, "Um… yes actually I did, the Shopkeeper was with the gardener and his son the night of the old lady's murder" Officer Smith still a bit surprised by the detectives general interest carries on "the only other thing I noticed was as I left the shopkeepers house to head back to the station, the window cleaner was standing outside the pub, I don't know how long he'd been there but it looked like he'd been watching the house".

The detective took in everything Officer Smith had to say in, "So the shopkeeper has confirmed what the gardener told us in his interview," and decided to inform Officer Smith of what he had found out from the Old Lady's letter. The detective explains how he believes the gardener is innocent as he has a strong alibi for the old lady's murder and even though he doesn't have one for the first murder, the gardener doesn't have a motive or a reason to kill the mother of his child. This is one thing the detective and Officer Smith can both agree on but where does it leave them with the other three suspects?

Officer Smith is sitting, listening to the detective explain what was in the old lady's letter and how even though the detective isn't ruling anything out, the detective is 99% certain that the murderer is the window cleaner and they just need a motive and the evidence to back it up.

Officer Smith tells the detective, "It sounds to me the motive is revenge on the gardener as you anticipated at the start of the investigation." Both Officer Smith and the detective agree on the motive. Officer Smith continues, "The window cleaner kills the old lady because he thinks she saw him" another admission both the detective and Officer Smith agree on. They decide to focus just on the window cleaner, Officer Smith decides to make a list.

- Doesn't have an alibi for either murder
- Has an agender against the gardener (wants revenge)
- Was seen leaving the victim's house time of the murder

The detective said, "All that shows is that he's guilty, we still don't have the murder weapon and it still leaves a lot of questions unanswered officer". Officer Smith looks at the detective and replies, "It leaves us with a clear path, the shopkeeper is hiding something, so we re-interview her and then her mother the pub owner if we have to." The detective nods their head, and looks at Officer Smith and says "sounds like a plan, let's interview the shopkeeper first and find out what she's kept back from us and what that conversation was about between her and her mother, that you overheard".

Officer Smith agrees and gets right onto re-interviewing the shopkeeper, what is she holding back from the detective?

Chapter 8
Truth and Fear

The next day Officer Smith has arranged to interview the shopkeeper again. While waiting for the shopkeeper to arrive at the station. Officer Smith decides to have a look through the report of the old lady's murder and read the letter she left for the detective.

After reading the letter for themselves Officer Smith's point of view differs from the detectives slightly, Officer Smith wonders whether despite the shopkeeper having an alibi for the time of the old lady's murder was the one that killed the victim and her brother the window cleaner realising what his sister was going to do went to house that night to stop her but was too late and as he left saw that the old lady had possible witnessed the event and in protecting his sister killed the old lady.

Officer Smith decides to put this theory to the detective before they go and interview the shopkeeper. After hearing the officer out the detective agrees with Officer Smith and says that it is a possibility that could be the case but due to the window cleaner's lack of evidence as well as having no alibi for both murders, he is as of now the prime suspect but that could change depending on what more they can get out of the shopkeeper and if she's willing to tell the truth.

Both the detective and Officer Smith are informed that the shopkeeper has arrived for her interview but the officer hesitates before telling them that the shopkeeper hasn't come alone. The detective asks who has accompanied the shopkeeper to which the officer replies that it's her mother the pub owner and that she has requested to be in the room, while you interview her daughter. "I bet she has," Officer Smith says with an aggressive tone in her voice while standing with her arms crossed. The detective just smirks and tells the officer, "inform the pub owner that if she wishes to give an interview herself will be happy to provide an interviewing room for her to wait in, otherwise she will be staying in the waiting area by reception until we are finished". The officer leaves to deliver the detective's message to the pub owner, whether she likes it or not is another matter but the detective doesn't care. On their way down to interview the shopkeeper hopefully for the final time, the detective and Officer Smith discuss what it is they need to know in order to be able to arrest and possibly charge her brother. she's probably not going to want to get him into trouble and also the fact that she's probably been under a lot of pressure from her mother to keep quiet and not say anything hasn't helped. As they arrive at the interviewing room, the officer who told the detective the shopkeeper had arrived along with her mother is waiting outside the interviewing room for the detective. The detective asks what's going on to which the officer tells the detective that the pub owner is in the room with her daughter. The detective is not happy, in fact, the detective is furious by this and asks how this happened when he gave strict instructions for that not to happen, the officer informs the detective that by the time they got back to deliver the detective's message a different officer had already placed the shopkeeper and her mother in the interviewing room. The detective looks at Officer Smith and says, "What are we going to do now… there's no way she's going to talk with her mother in there with her." Officer Smith tries to calm the detective down and comes up with an idea but knows they going to need someone else's help to get the pub owner out of the way, "I have an idea, it's a bit made but I think it'll work" the detective at this point will try anything and agrees "OK, whatever your plan is let's do it and do it fast".

Officer Smith tells the officer next to her to come up with a reason to get the pub owner out of the interviewing room and back to the village to which the officer hesitates at first but then agrees to help once he understands that it's to help find out who killed the victim. Officer Smith returns and tells the detective the plan, the detective isn't sure about this plan but trusts Officer Smith, so agrees to go along with it and that's when they enter the room to start the interview. Officer Smith explains, that after she visited the shopkeeper a couple of days ago, they need what the shopkeeper said about having an alibi for the old lady's murder put on record. The pub owner turns around and says, "Is that all you called my daughter here for." The detective responds, "You're here as an observer, not a participant, so please keep quiet" The shopkeeper just shrugs her shoulders and says, "If that's what this is all about then, OK". As the shopkeeper was finishing giving her alibi on the night of the old lady's murder of where she was and who she was with, one of the officers comes into the interviewing room, "Sorry detective, we've received a message for the pub owner, the security alarms have gone off at the pub", the pub owner rolling her eyes "something had to happen didn't it" she looked at the shopkeeper before saying "you'll be fine, just remember what I said" the pub owner leaves. After the pub owner has gone the detective informs the shopkeeper of why she's really there and what it is they need to know. Officer Smith also tells the shopkeeper that at this moment in time, she is a suspect which comes as a huge shock and surprise to the shopkeeper. The detective starts by saying, "We have evidence that proves you were at home the same time your brother returned, what kind of mood was he in?" The shopkeeper answers, "The usually, a bad one, blaming the gardener for everything, telling me I'm not to be with the victim… I questioned whether it was my brother who killed her, after all, I did provoke him by telling him that we were leaving the village." Officer Smith jumps in, "You know you're safe here, you can tell us the truth, there's no need to be afraid". The shopkeeper looking very fearful of saying too much and worried about her mother coming back, asks if the interview is over and if can she leave. The detective realises that the shopkeeper has had the fear of god put in her to make sure she won't talk, so the detective decides the only way to get the truth out of the shopkeeper, while they have her on her own is to tell her the truth of who they believe is the killer and why.

"I'm going to lay it all down on the table for you, I am 100% sure that the murderer is your brother but at this precise moment in time all I have is a letter of evidence left by the old lady confirming that he left the victim's house at 11:40 pm around the time of the murder" the shopkeeper looking straight at the detective nervously "what that means is with this letter which also confirms nobody else entered the house around the time of the murder, that the only people who could've committed it, is you or your brother". The shopkeeper pleads her innocence and Officer Smith responds "you can plead your innocence all you want but unless you tell us the truth of what happened that night, in our minds you're guilty". The shopkeeper with her head in her hands decides to come clean but makes it clear to the detective that she never wanted to lie or keep it from them but that her brother is very controlling. The detective and Officer Smith listened as the shopkeeper explained how they had spent the first half an hour packing and decided to take a break. The victim made them both drinks and they were sat on the sofa discussing the new house when there was a knock on the door, the shopkeeper explained how it was her that answered the door and was surprised to see that it was her brother and explained how he pushed her out the way and went straight into the living room and started attacking the victim while shouting about how it was all the gardeners fault and how he deserved this and everything else that was coming to him and he was the reason as to why his life was so miserable. The Shopkeeper didn't know her brother had a knife on him until she tried to get him off the victim and got cut on her arm, she tells the detective how her brother started walking towards her and how she thought she was next, so she ran out the back door and went and hid in the shed and waited until she thought he might've gone. The shopkeeper explained as soon as she re-enter the house she called for the police and that she already knew the victim had died, "I was just glad that the little boy wasn't in the house that night". The detective and Officer Smith knows they have what they need to arrest the window cleaner for the murder of the victim but not the old lady and asks the shopkeeper if she knows anything about where her mother and brother were during that night. The shopkeeper tells the detective as far as she knows her mother was working as one of the bar girls had phoned in sick, as for her brother she didn't know but wouldn't be surprised if it wasn't him. After the interview is finished, on their way out the detective offers the shopkeeper police protection to which the shopkeeper politely declines and says, "Thank you detective but I've made it this far without it, I'm sure I'll be just fine on my own" the detective tells the shopkeeper not to hesitate to call if she needs them before heading back up to their office. Once back upstairs at the office, the detective and Officer Smith discuss what to do next and how to handle the situation. The detective asks Officer Smith to inform every one of the developments while he tells their superior officer that they have their murderer. The detective returns to inform Officer Smith that they are to go to the village to find and arrest the window cleaner. What will they find and will the window cleaner be expecting them?

Chapter 9
Hide and Seek

Once they arrive back in the village the detective orders officers with them to search the places where the Window Cleaner is mostly likely to be, "Officer Smith, take some officers with you and search the house, the rest of you I want to go and search the pub and remember we're not just here for the window cleaner we're here for his mother as well" the detective tells the officers "what you waiting for, go" the detective orders.

Officer Smith goes to the house and knocks on the door, the shopkeeper answers and asks what the officer is doing there, "I have a warrant to search these premises, we are looking for your brother." The shopkeeper complies and lets Officer Smith and the other officers in. Inside the house, some officers head upstairs to search Officer Smith searches downstairs and asks the shopkeeper when she last saw her brother to which the shopkeeper replies, "Last night, he went out after eight and never came back." Officer Smith questions the shopkeeper's answer about her brother's whereabouts to which the shopkeeper replies sternly, "If I wasn't telling the truth officer, I would not have given the interview I gave yesterday would I" Officer Smith backs off and shouts to the other officers in the house asking if they've found anything, to which each respond with negative officer. Officer Smith decides to call the officers back and leave the shopkeeper's house, "Thank you for your time." Officer Smith says to the shopkeeper as they leave the house.

Over at the pub, the officers have arrived to search for the window cleaner and to arrest the pub owner. As they enter, the pub owner is sitting at one of the tables with the gardener sitting opposite her, "Oh, look who's arrived… just in time too," says the pub owner. The detective standing there in the doorway looks at both of them and then sees that the gardener is holding a knife, the detective quickly gets the officers to arrest the pub owner and take her outside out of the way as well as gently removing the knife from the gardeners hand and putting it out of reach. As the pub owner is escorted out the detective sits opposite him. The gardener is visibly upset and angry, the detective asks the gardener what the pub owner told him, to which he replies "she told me, she killed the victim because she thought I was going to leave the village with her and start over, especially with her having the baby on the way." The detective shaking his head, leans forward and tells the gardener that what the pub owner has told him isn't true and that it wasn't her who killed the victim, it was her son the Window Cleaner out of revenge for his father being in prison and his sister wanting to leave the village as well as his relationship with his mother. The gardener looking back at the detective can't believe what he's hearing but to some degree wasn't surprised either I knew it was him from the start, especially after his mother became so protective of him." The gardener continues, "I can't believe she choose to protect him after everything he's done," the detective interrupts the gardener, "I need you tell me something, do you think the pub owner killed the old lady?" the gardener thinking about the detectives question as well as the night in question answers "it's a possibility, she worked that night because one of the bar girls phoned in sick but I don't recall her ever coming upstairs once the pub closed and the window cleaner hadn't been seen at all that day" the detective asks the gardener one final question before they leave "do you know where the window cleaner is now?" the gardener replies "no, I don't but you better find him before I do" The detective stands up and walks out of the pub leaving the gardener behind. Outside the officer is putting the pub owner in the back of the police car, the detective walks over to her "you hear to charge me detective, after all I confess to murdering the victim and the old lady" the detective replies "Is that right, the victim maybe but how did you do it with the old lady" the pub owner explains how she waited until after closing at the pub so she'd have an alibi before going over and killing the old lady, the pub owner laughing in victory, convinced that she's got her son of the hook as well as gotten away with killing the old lady because she's confessed to the detective only for the detective to turn round and say "then yes I am charging you" Officer Smith looks at the detective surprised "but not with the murder of the victim, for the murder of the old lady" the pub owner shocked by this turns nasty and says to the detective how they can't do this, how they have no evidence. The detective looks at the officer and tells them to take her away. After the pub owner is driven away the detective and Officer Smith stand outside the pub looking towards the village and wondering where the window cleaner might be hiding. They know he's somewhere in the village but where.

Officer Smith says, "There's only two places left he could be." The detective looking at the victim's house knows that's where he is and decides to send Officer Smith with a group of officers over to the old lady's house and the detective decides to go and find the window cleaner. As they make their way over the detective orders the officers with them to surround the house outside and to cover all exits, the detective decides to enter the house alone. The detective walks slowly up to the front door and sees that it has been opened, he enters the house slowly and cautiously, knowing that the window cleaner is in there somewhere.

Once the detective has entered he slowly walks down the hallway towards the entrance to the living room where the murder took place, once there he looks through the doorway into the living room and sees the window cleaner standing looking down at where the victim's body once was and at the blood stains that remain on the carpet. "I knew you'd find me eventually detective," the window cleaner says as if he knew the detective was coming for him, "a moment of madness and everything changed that night and then things only got worse." The detective slowly walks into the living room, "We both know it wasn't a moment of madness" the detective replies as he walks around the room slowly until he is standing opposite the window cleaner. The window cleaner opens up to the detective telling him how he never meant to kill the victim and how it was an accident but the detective isn't buying any of it, the window cleaner is standing in the house in the exact room and even in the exact spot the murder took place and has no emotion no remorse, the detective feels like they are looking at someone who either has no idea of what they have done or someone who is just Pure evil and wants to see the results of his crime one final time knowing the game is over he's finally been caught.

Outside Officer Smith returns from her search of the old lady's house and asks one of the officers where the detective is they say that the detective is inside the house alone. Officer Smith decides to slowly enter with two other officers as they get to the living room entrance they can see that the window cleaner has his back to them and the detective is talking to him trying to get information out of him about the night of the murder.

The detective continues knowing that Officer Smith is right behind the window cleaner. "What about the old lady, did you kill her?" the window cleaner starts laughing at the detective, "Why would I want to waste my time and kill that noisy old cow." The window cleaner replies the detective realises that the window cleaner doesn't know the old lady saw him the night of the murder and decides to tell him to see his reaction, "because she saw you kill the victim and gave evidence against you before she was murdered" the window cleaner stops laughing and looks straight at the detective and realises that the detective isn't playing with him and is telling the truth. The window cleaner starts to panic and decides to try and make a run for it but as he does he runs straight into Officer Smith and the other officers right behind him. The window cleaner doesn't give up without a fight and the officers have to restrain him on the floor so they can handcuff him and arrest him. Once the window cleaner is arrested for the victim's murder he's taken outside to be put in the back of the police car and taken back to the station. Outside Officer

Smith asks the detective if the window cleaner didn't murder the old lady then does that mean they have to separate murders, the detective explains to Officer Smith how they have both murderers in custardy and the evidence to charge them both, Officer Smith looks at the detective confused and says "we have the evidence to charge the window cleaner but we don't have the evidence to charge the pub owner" the detective just walks away and says to Officer Smith, I'll see you back at the station". The detective leaves, leaving Officer Smith confused and with more questions, what did the detective know or have that could prove the pub owner guilty of murdering the old lady and their evidence to charge the window cleaner relied on the old lady's letter as well as his sister's evidence. Has the detective finally found the knife used to kill the victim if so how?

Chapter 10
Truth Will Out

The detective along with Officer Smith are sat in one of the interviewing rooms opposite the Window Cleaner. With the interview about to begin the window cleaner is sat looking dishevelled and emotionless, looking over at the detective almost like he's looking through the detective. As the detective starts the window cleaner immediately responds with a no comment, so the detective decides to tell the window cleaner how he thinks the murder happened and why.

The detective starts with his mother's affair and how it not only split his parents up but is the reason his father is in prison. The detective talks about the way the window cleaner witnessed his mother, in his eyes be used and embarrassed by the gardener, but the one thing the window cleaner was bothered about the most was how he and his mother didn't like his sister's relationship with the victim and how they were leaving the village to start over. The detective carries on, but what tips you over the edge is when you find out your mother has got back together with the gardener, it's what led you to stay away from the pub and over the next few weeks leading up to the murder, every time you saw them together it made you angry and so you decided to get revenge on the gardener for splitting your family apart. The night you murdered your sister's partner, you did it after you returned from visiting your father. You got back about ten and you waited till you knew everyone in the village would either be at home or at the pub and then you walked over to the house, you got there at eleven thirty, your sister answered the door, after the two of you had argued earlier that night she was surprised to see you but you didn't care you forced your way past, pushing your sister over and went straight into the living room and attacked the victim. You cut your sister's arm when she tried to get you off the victim but out of fear that you were going to kill her, she ran out the back and locked herself in the shed.

Once you've killed the victim you leave, but as you walk out through the front door you forget all about the old lady sitting looking through her bedroom window, who's just witnessed you entering and leaving the house. A few days later after being interviewed by myself and Officer Smith, you realise that you can't risk us getting to the old lady before you, but you underestimated the old lady as she knew you were coming for her and she got one step ahead of you and wrote down everything she saw that night, which she knew can still be used as evidence, she hid the letter under her chair and waited for you to come and you did.

The window cleaner just nods and says, "You have no evidence to prove this, yes you have the old lady's letter which proves I was at the victim's house but without the murder weapon, all you have is a theory and that's it". Officer Smith informs the window cleaner that his sister gave evidence yesterday confirming everything the detective has just said. The window cleaner shocked that his own sister would turn on him tells both the detective and Officer Smith.

"You might have witnesses but you still don't have a murder weapon" The detective looks at the window cleaner and asks him to remove his boots to which the window cleaner refuses, the detective angry and out of patience says, "Remove your boots or my officers will do it for you", the window cleaner realising he can't get out of it and has nowhere to go, removes his boots. The detective puts on a pair of gloves lifts up the left boot and turns it upside down to which nothing comes out, the detective then does the same with the right boot and out drops a knife, a pen knife which the detective opens up and sees that it is covered in blood.

The detective puts the knife in a bag and hands it to Officer Smith and proceeds to arrest and charge the window cleaner with the victim's murder. The last thing the window cleaner says is how the victim deserved what she got and how the gardener has to live with it, the detective responds in anger towards the window cleaner and says, "You killed an innocent woman and her unborn child in cold blood out of revenge for a situation that had nothing to do her, the only person who has to live with this is you, while you spend the rest of your life behind bars", the window cleaner suddenly waking up and realising what he has done as the detective says to the officers "take him away" the officers escort the Window cleaner out and down to the cells.

The detective goes to the next room where the pub owner is waiting, the detective takes a seat and looks at the pub owner who's rigged with guilt and says, "You knew didn't you, all this time and you knew." The pub owner leaning over the table looking at the detective, begs him, "Say it was me, he didn't mean it, it was a moment of madness, he didn't know what he was doing, please say it was me." The detective looking back at the pub owner with a little bit of pity for her just says, "I can't do that, your son has killed an innocent woman and her unborn child, he must pay the price for it." The detective continues, "But the one thing you can do is tell me the truth about where you were that night."

The pub owner starts by saying, "I don't see the point, it's not going to change anything but if that's what you want." The pub owner then explains how she went to change the barrels pushing half eleven, after she finished with that she decided to take the rubbish out and how it was then she found out what her son had done, "I turned around to go back into the pub and he was stood there with blood on his hands, I asked him what had he'd done and he told me, he told me how he stabbed the victim and how his sister caught him and how he accidentally cut her arm when he tried to stop her running from him."

The detective shakes his head in disbelief as Officer Smith tells the pub owner, "This could've been over long ago, if you had just told us the truth and only one murder would've been committed not two but you chose to try and get the gardener charged with murder", "all of this was an act of revenge based on your affair and you can blame the gardener all you want but it takes two to create an affair and now you have to live with the fact that not only is your son a murderer and has killed two people but that, the victim's son is going to grow up without his mother" the detective interrupts by saying "your son didn't kill the old lady though did he" the pub owner shakes her head at the detective and confesses to killing the old lady to protect her son.

After hearing the pub owner's confession the detective charges her with murder and ends the interview, the detective tells the officer to take the pub owner away.

Now that it is all over and they have both murders in custardy the detective decides to go back to the village and see the gardener one last time. Officer Smith decides to go with the detective, as they arrive there is a removal van outside the pub, the detective stops the car and gets out along with Officer Smith and walks over to the gardener who is standing talking to the shopkeeper outside the pub. The detective walks up to them and asks what going on, to which the gardener informs the detective that he has decided to leave and move into the house the victim intended to move to.

Officer Smith looks at the shopkeeper and asks her what she intends to do, the shopkeeper insists that she's going to sell the pub and the house but after that, she's not sure, the gardener's son who has appeared from nowhere speaks for the first time since his mother's death and asks the shopkeeper to go with him and his dad to the new house to start over. The gardener looks down at his son then looks up at the shopkeeper, smiles and says, "He's right, you can come with us if you want." The shopkeeper smiles back and agrees, the detective and Officer Smith wish them luck and leave to head back to the station.

On their way back Officer Smith tells the detective how much they enjoyed working with him despite the circumstances, the detective smirks and says, "It was nice working with you too… Sargent Smith." Officer Smith looks over at the detective in shock, "Sargent, did you just call me Sargent?" The detective informs Officer Smith that due to their hard work and dedication throughout this case, she has now been appointed Sargent Smith. While the newly appointed Sargent Smith celebrates her new role on the drive back there are questions that remain, What's next for the detective? Is there another case on the horizon? Who knows? but one thing is for certain life's always a game of Guess Who?